Enid Blyton

A FARAWAY TREE
Adventure

The Land of
SILLY SCHOOL

For Thomas and Isabel
A. P.

EGMONT

We bring stories to life

Cover and interior illustrations by Alex Paterson

Text first published in Great Britain as chapters 13–14
of *The Folk of the Faraway Tree* 1946
Published as *The Land of Silly School: A Faraway Tree Adventure* 2017
by Egmont UK Limited
2 Minster Court, 10th floor, London EC3R 7BB

ISBN 978 1 4052 8605 3

www.egmont.co.uk

A CIP catalogue record for this title is available from the British Library

Printed in Singapore

66576/003

Enid Blyton

A FARAWAY TREE
Adventure

The Land of
SILLY SCHOOL

EGMONT

The World of the
FARAWAY TREE

MOON-FACE lives at the very top. In his house is the start of the **SLIPPERY-SLIP**, a huge slide that curves all the way down inside the trunk of the tree.

SILKY lives below Moon-Face. She is the prettiest little fairy you ever did see.

SAUCEPAN MAN is a funny old thing. His saucepans make lots of noise when they jangle together, so he can't hear very well.

CHAPTER ONE
Off to Dame Snap's School

One day, a message came from Moon-Face. 'I have heard from Saucepan. He says we must go up to Dame Snap's Land tomorrow, and meet his mother. If we go to the back door of **Dame Snap's** school, she will be there.'

So the next day, the four children set off.

They went up the Faraway Tree, and called for
Silky first. She was wearing a pretty party dress,
and had washed her hair, which looked more
like a **golden mist** than ever.

'I'm just ready,' she said, giving her hair a

last brush. 'I hope Moon-Face won't keep us waiting. He lost his hat this morning, and he's been **rushing up and down** the tree all day, asking everyone if they've seen it.'

When they got to Moon-Face's he was quite ready, **beaming** as usual, a floppy hat on his head.

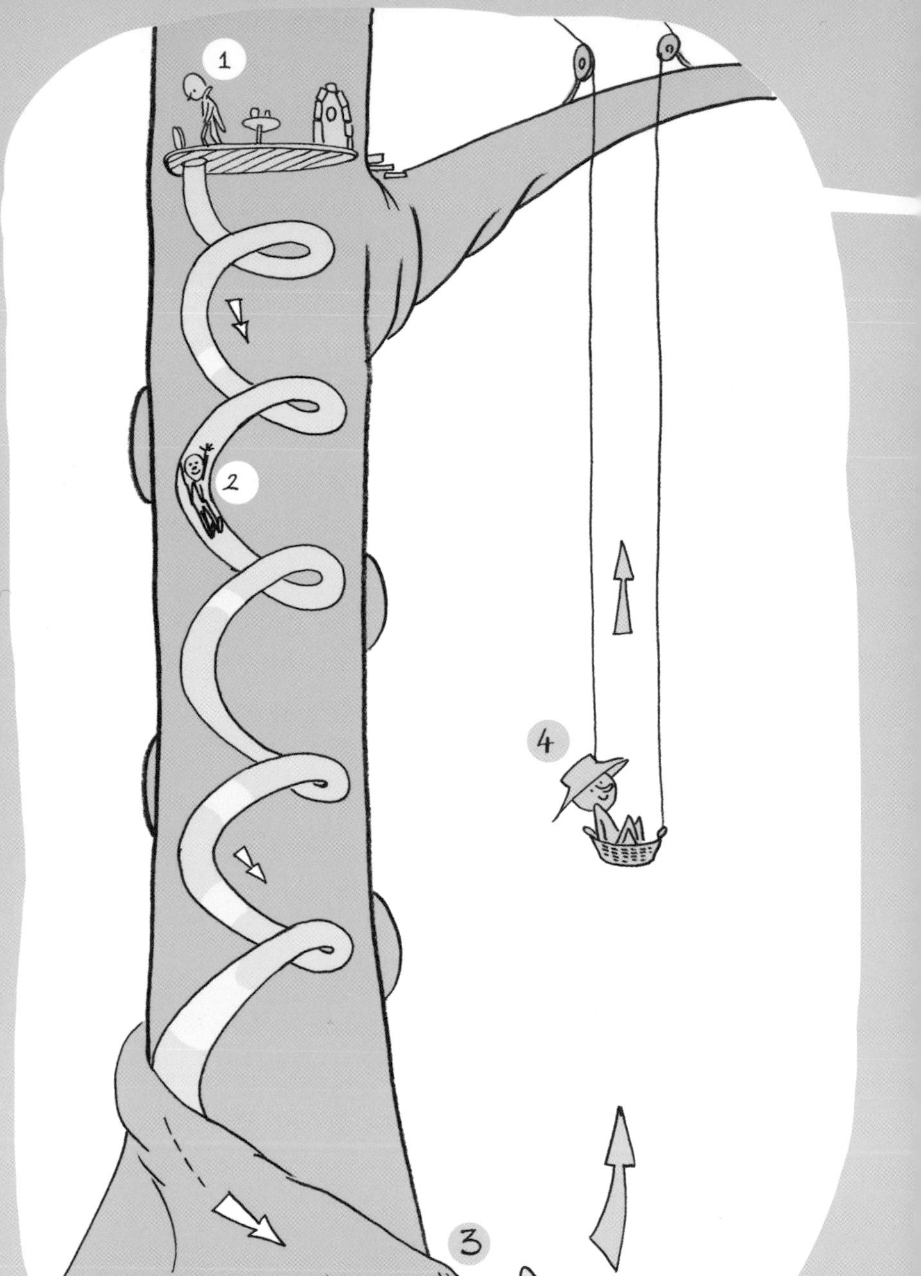
1
2
3
4

'Oh, you **found** your hat then?' said Silky.

'Yes – it had fallen down the slippery-slip,' said Moon-Face. 'And when I went down there, **I shot out** of the trapdoor at the bottom, and there was my hat on my feet! So that was all right. Are we all ready?'

'Yes,' said Joe. 'But for goodness' sake do look out for Dame Snap. **I feel very nervous** of her.'

'Saucepan will be looking out for us, don't worry,' said Moon-Face. 'I expect he will be at the top of the ladder, waiting. We're sure to have a lovely meal. His mother is **a wonderful cook**.'

5

They **climbed up** the topmost branch of the tree, and came to the ladder. They all went up it and found themselves in Dame Snap's Land. There wasn't much to see – only, in the distance, a large green house set in the middle of a great garden.

'That's **Dame Snap's School**,' said Joe to Connie.

'Who goes to it?' asked Connie, **curiously**.
'All the **bad pixies and fairies and elves**,' said Beth. 'We saw some once when we were there. Dame Snap has to be very strict or she wouldn't be able to teach them. They are very naughty.'

'Where's the back door?' said Connie, **looking nervously around**. 'Let's go there, quick. I do wish Saucepan had waited for us at the top of the ladder.

'Yes, I don't know why he didn't,' said Moon-Face, **puzzled**. 'Shall we call him?'

'No, of course not, silly!' said Joe. 'We'll have Dame Snap **after us at once!** Come on –

we'll find the back door. We really can't wait

about any longer.'

So they went round the large garden,

keeping **carefully** outside the high wall, until

they came to two gates. One opened on to

the drive that led to the front door. The other

opened on to a path that clearly led to the

back door.

'This is where we go,' said Beth, and they went quietly through the back gate. They came to the back door. **It was shut**. No one seemed to be about.

'I suppose Saucepan and his mother are expecting us?' said Joe, puzzled. He knocked on the door. **There was no answer**. He knocked again.

'Let's open the door and go in,' said Beth, impatiently. 'We must find Saucepan. I expect he's **forgotten** he asked us to come today.'

They pushed the door open and went into
a big and very tidy kitchen. There was no one
there. **It was very strange**. Connie opened
another door and peered into what seemed to
be a big hall.

'I think **I can hear someone**,' she said. 'I'll go and see if it's Saucepan.'

Before the others could stop her she had opened the door and gone. No one **felt like following**. They sat down in the kitchen and waited.

CHAPTER TWO
A Surprise for Curious Connie

Connie went into the big hall. There was no one there. She went into another room, that looked like a living room. **Connie peered round it in curiosity**. Then, through a door opposite came a tall, old woman, with large spectacles on her long nose and a big white bonnet on her head.

'Oh!' said Connie, beaming. '**Happy birthday!** Where's Saucepan? We've all come to meet you!'

The old woman stopped in surprise.

'**Indeed!**' she said. 'You have, have you? And who are the rest of you?'

'**Oh – didn't Saucepan tell you?**' asked Connie. 'There's Joe and Beth and Frannie and Moon-Face and Silky. We did hope that Saucepan would meet us by the ladder,

because we were so afraid of meeting that
awful Dame Snap.'

'Oh, really?' said the old woman, and **her
eyes gleamed** behind her big spectacles. 'You
think she's awful, do you?'

'Well, Joe and the others told me all about her,' said Connie. 'They were all here once, you know, and **they escaped**. They were very afraid of meeting her again.'

'**Where are they?**' said the old woman.

'**In the kitchen**,' said Connie. 'I'll go and tell them I've found you.'

She ran ahead of the old woman, who followed her at once. **Connie flung open the kitchen door.**

'I've found Saucepan's mother!' she said. **'Here she is!'**

The old lady came into the kitchen – and Joe and the others **gave a gasp of horror**. It wasn't Saucepan's mother. It was Dame Snap herself, looking absolutely furious.

'Dame Snap!' yelled Joe. **'Run, everyone!'**

But **it was too late**. Dame Snap turned the key in the kitchen door and put it into her pocket.

CHAPTER THREE
Back to School

'**So you escaped from me before, did you?**' she said. 'Well, you won't escape again. Bad children who are sent to me to be good don't usually escape before they are taught

things they ought to know!'

'**Look here!**' began Moon-Face, putting a bold face on. 'Look here, Dame Snap, we didn't come to see you; we came to see Saucepan's mother.'

'I've never in my life heard of Saucepan,' said Dame Snap. '**Never. It's a naughty story.** You're making it up. I punish people for telling stories. You wicked man!' she snapped at Moon-Face.

'Saucepan's mother works for you!' he shouted, dodging round the kitchen. '**She cooks for your school!** Where is she?'

25

26

'Oh – the lady who cooks,' said Dame Snap. 'Well, she walked out yesterday, along with a **dreadful creature** who had kettles and pans hung all round him.'

'**That was Saucepan**,' groaned Joe. 'Where did they go?'

'I don't know and I certainly don't care,' said Dame Snap. 'The lady was rude to me, and I shouted at her. So she went off. **Can any of you cook?**'

'I can,' said Beth. 'But if you think I'm going to cook for you, you're mistaken. **I'm going home**.'

'You can stay here and cook meals for the school till I get someone else,' said Dame Snap. **'And this girl can help you.'** She pointed to Frannie. 'The others can come into my school and learn to work hard, to get good manners and to be well behaved. Go along now!'

28

To Joe's horror, she pushed everyone but Beth and Frannie into the hall, and up the stairs to a big classroom, where **lots of noisy little elves, fairies and pixies** were playing and pushing and fighting together.

Dame Snap dealt a few scoldings

and sent them to their seats, yelling.

Connie was very afraid. She stayed close to Joe and Moon-Face. Dame Snap made them all sit down at the back of the room.

'**Silence!**' she snapped. 'You will now do your homework. The new pupils will please find pencils and paper in their desks. Everyone must answer the questions on the blackboard. If anyone gets them wrong, they will have to be punished.'

'**Oh dear!**' groaned Silky. Connie whispered to her:

'**Don't worry!** I'm very good at lessons. I will know all the answers, and I'll tell you them too.'

'**Who is whispering?**' shouted Dame Snap, and everyone jumped. 'You, new girl, come out here.'

Connie came out, trembling. Dame Snap gave her a sharp scolding.

'**Stop crying!**' she snapped. And Connie stopped. She gave a gulp, and stopped at once.

'Go back to your seat and **do your homework**,' ordered the old Dame. So back Connie went.

'**Now, no talking and no playing**,' said Dame Snap. 'Just hard work. I am going to talk to my new kitchen staff about a nice syrup pudding. If I hear anyone talking or playing when I come back, or if anyone hasn't done the homework, there will be no nice syrup pudding for any of you.'

35

With this threat Dame Snap walked out of
the room. She left the door **wide open** so that
she could hear any noise.

The pixie in front of Connie turned round and shook his pen on her book. A big blot came out! The goblin next to him **pulled Silky's hair.** A bright-eyed pixie threw a pencil at Moon-Face and hit him on the nose. Dame Snap's pupils were a really naughty lot!

'**We must do our homework!**' whispered Silky to the others. 'Connie, read the questions on the blackboard, and tell us the answers, quick!'

So Connie read them — but, oh dear, how could she answer questions like that? She never could. They would all go without syrup pudding, and **be scolded and sent to bed!** Oh dear, oh dear!

40

CHAPTER FOUR
Very Silly Questions

The more the children looked at the three questions on the blackboard, the more they felt certain they could never answer them. Moon-Face turned to Connie. **'Quick! Tell us the right answers.** You said you were good at lessons.'

Connie read the first question. 'Three blackbirds sat on a cherry tree. They ate one hundred and twenty-three of the cherries. **How many were left?'**

'Well, how can we say, unless we know
how many there were in the beginning?' said
Connie, out loud. **'What a silly question!'**

Joe read the next one out loud. 'If there are
a hundred pages in a book, how many books
would there be on the shelf?'

'**The questions are just nonsense**,' said Moon-Face, gloomily.

'They were before, when we were here,' said Joe.

The third question was very short. Joe read it out. '**Why is a blackboard?**'

43

'Why is a blackboard!' repeated Silky. '**There is no sense** in that question either.'

'Well – the questions are **nonsense**, so we'll put down answers that are nonsense,' said Joe.

So they put down '**none**' about how many cherries were left on the tree. Then they read the book question again. And again they put down '**none**'.

'We are not told that the shelf was a book shelf,' said Joe. 'It might be a shelf for ornaments, or a bathroom shelf for glasses and toothbrushes and things. **There wouldn't be any books there.**'

The third question was really puzzling. '**Why is a blackboard?**'

Joe ran out of his place and rubbed out the two last words. He wrote them again – and then the question read 'Why is a board black?'

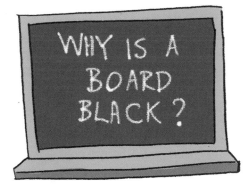

'We can easily answer that,' said Joe, with a grin. 'Why is a board black? **So that we can write on it with white chalk!**'

So, when Dame Snap came back, the only people who had answered all the questions were Joe, Silky, Moon-Face and Connie! Dame Snap smiled at them. **'Dear me, I have some clever children at last!'** she said. 'You have written answers to all the questions.'

'Are they right then?' asked Silky, in surprise.

'I don't know,' said Dame Snap. '**But that doesn't matter**. It's the answers I want. I don't care what's in them, so long as you have written answers. I don't know the answers myself, so it's no good me reading them.'

Then Moon-Face undid all the good they had done by giving an extremely rude snort. 'Pooh! What a silly school this is! Fancy giving people questions if you don't know the answers! **Pooh!**'

'Don't "pooh" at me like that!' said Dame Snap, getting angry all of a sudden. '**Go to bed!** Off to bed with you for the rest of the day!'

'But – but,' began poor Moon-Face, in alarm, wishing he had not spoken, '**but . . .**'

'**You'll turn into a
goat in a minute**, if you
are so full of "buts",' said
Dame Snap, and she pushed
Moon-Face out of the door.

She drove the others out too, and took them to
a small bedroom, with four tiny beds, very hard
and narrow.

CHAPTER FIVE

A Song to the Rescue

'**Now, into bed you get,** and nothing but bread and water for you all day long. I will not have rudeness in my school!'

She shut the door and locked it. Moon-Face looked at the others in dismay. '**I'm sorry** I made her do this,' he said. 'Very sorry. But really, **she did make me feel so angry**. Do you think we'd better go to bed? She might punish us if we don't.'

Connie leapt into bed at once, fully dressed. She wasn't going to risk Dame Snap coming back and punishing her! The others did the same. They drew the quilts up to their chins and **lay there gloomily**. This was a horrid adventure – just when they had looked forward so much to coming out to the birthday party.

'I wonder what Beth and Frannie are doing,' said Moon-Face. '**Hard work, I suppose**. I do think Saucepan might have warned us that his mother had gone. **It's too bad**.'

Just then there came the sound of a song floating up from outside.

'Two worms for a **sparrow**,
Two slugs for a **duck**,
Two snails for a **blackbird**,
Two hens for a **cluck!**'

'**Saucepan!** It must be Saucepan!' cried everyone, and jumped out of bed and ran to the window. Outside, far below, stood Saucepan, and with him were Beth and Frannie, giggling.

'Hi, Saucepan! Here we are!' cried Joe. **'We're locked in.'**

'Oh – we wondered where you were,' said Saucepan, grinning. **'Dame Snap's locked in, too** – locked into the store room by young Beth here. She was just doing it when I came along to see if you had arrived.'

'Arrived! **We've been here ages**,' said Joe, indignantly. 'Why didn't you come to warn us?'

'My watch must be wrong again,' said Saucepan. He usually kept it in one of his kettles, but as it shook about there every day, it wasn't a very good time keeper. 'Never mind. **I'll rescue you now**.'

A terrific banging noise came from somewhere downstairs. 'That's Dame Snap in the store room,' said Saucepan. **'She's in a dreadful temper.'**

'Well, for goodness' sake, help us out of here,' said Connie, alarmed. 'How can we get out? The door's locked, and I heard Dame Snap taking the key out the other side.'

Crash! Bang! Clatter!

'Sounds as if Dame Snap is throwing a few pies and things about,' said Joe. '**Saucepan, how can we get out of here?**'

'I'll just undo the rope that hangs my things round me,' said Saucepan, and he began to untie the rope round his waist. He undid it, and then, to the children's surprise, **his kettles and saucepans began to peel off him.** They were each tied firmly to the rope.

'Saucepan does look funny without his kettles and pans round him,' said Connie in surprise. '**I hardly know him!**'

Saucepan took the end of the rope and tied a stone to it. He threw it up to the window. Joe caught the stone and **pulled on the rope**. It came up, laden here and there with kettles and saucepans.

'Tie the rope end to a bed,' called Saucepan. 'Then come down the rope. You can use the kettles and saucepans as steps. They are tied on tightly.'

So, **very cautiously**, Moon-Face, Joe, Silky and a very nervous Connie climbed down the rope, using the saucepans and kettles as steps. They were very glad to stand on firm ground again!

'Well, there we are,' said Saucepan, pleased. **'Wasn't that a good idea?'**

'Yes – **but how** are we to get your kettles and saucepans back for you?' said Joe.

'**It doesn't matter at all**,' said Saucepan. 'I can take as many as I can carry out of the kitchen here. They are what I gave my mother each birthday, you know, so they are hers.'

He went into the kitchen and collected a
great selection of kettles and saucepans. He tied
them all to the rope used for a washing line,
and then once more became the Old Saucepan
Man they knew so well, with **pans of all
shapes and sizes hung all round him!**

CHAPTER SIX
A Lesson for Dame Snap

Crash! Smash! Clang! Dame Snap was getting angrier and angrier in the store room. She kicked and she stamped.

'Dame Snap!' cried Joe, suddenly, and he stood outside the locked store room door. 'I will ask you a question, and if you can tell me the answer, **I will set you free**. Now, be quiet and listen.'

There was a **silence** in the store room. Joe asked his question.

'If Saucepan takes **twelve kettles from your kitchen, how long does it take to boil** a cup of hot chocolate on a Friday?'

The others giggled. There came an angry cry from the store room. 'It's a silly question, and there's no answer. **Let me out at once!**'

'It's the same kind of question you asked us!' said Joe. 'I'm sorry you can't answer it. I can't either. So you must stay where you are, till one of your school children is kind enough to let you out. Goodbye, dear Dame Snap!'

The children and the others went out giggling into the garden. '**Where are we going now?**' asked Beth. 'Where's your mother, Saucepan?'

'She's in the Land of Tea Parties,' said Saucepan. 'It's not very far. I took her there because it's her birthday, you know, and I thought she'd like to have a party without going to any trouble. **Shall we go?**'

So, hearing Dame Snap's furious cries and bangs gradually fading behind them, the little group set off together, very glad to have escaped from Dame Snap in safety.

'**Come on** – here's the boundary between this land and the next. **Jump!**' said Saucepan.

They jumped – and over they went into the **Land of Tea Parties!** What a fine time they meant to have there!